COUNTRY BOY

Jim + Karen —

Hope you

enjoy

these

Jim Farfaglia

poems.

Jim Farfaglia

9/26/12

COUNTRY BOY by Jim Farfaglia

Copyright September 2011

All rights reserved. No part of this book may be reproduced
without the publisher's written permission, except for brief
quotations in reviews.

Printed in the United States of America

Cover art: Dee Marie. Photo from the private collection of Jim
Farfaglia

ISBN 9-780615-535807

For
Dad & Mom
and for
Nick & Carly

Acknowledgements

Dr. Nate Pritts

Kathy Andolina
Robert Comenole
The Downtown Writer's Center
Joanne Familo
Linda Knowles
Ginger Leotta
June MacArthur
Dee Marie
Maureen Moriarty
Geri Seward
Mary Slimmer
Elizabeth Twiddy

cover design by Dee Marie

CONTENTS

Spring Ahead

Each year begins the same.

On a day too early in the spring, I'll venture out into my garden, find a clump of last year's damp, rotting leaves and pull them aside, like I'm pulling aside the curtains of a Broadway premiere. I'll hover above this earthen stage, taking time for my eyes to adjust, having spent far too many months staring out over a white and drab landscape. Peering down in anticipation, I'll find exactly what it is I'm looking for.

Little messengers of life will be waiting in pale green, yellow and red: the first sprouts of the growing season. Some will keep close to the soil, not yet strong enough to reach for the sky. Others will be clustered together, needing each other to lean on through the final cold and dreary days. Some will stand alone, brave soldiers sent from below to investigate this new world.

I know better then to be looking this early. Here in upstate New York, spring comes slowly, the Great Lake Ontario gripping us a few extra depressing weeks. The lake is like an icebox that the shifting of the earth's tilt has unplugged, yet its chill continues to envelop us. Sometimes there's snow on Easter Sunday or Mother's Day, sometimes a freak storm blankets college graduations. It's part of the legend of living here and local supermarkets know how to cash in on this, selling potted spring flowers well before the first day of spring. People buy them up, set them on their kitchen tables and turn their backs on the windows of the world.

I prefer my first glimpse of spring to take place outside, wrapped in my coat, hat and scarf. It's always just a quick peek, knowing that these tender shoots need *their* winter coats a bit longer too. Surely, uncovering them now is risky behavior for the health of those future flowers, but doing so is important to *my* health, like the annual checkup I keep to assure myself everything is as it should be.

Pulling those leaves aside also puts me back in touch with my childhood roots, with my memories of being born and raised on a stretch of country road and of belonging to an extended family of muck farmers. Sweeping away those leaves is like sweeping away the years that have piled up between me, the country boy and me, the grown up. As my pile of memories grows deeper, so does my curiosity of those early years. How did my grandparents come to be farmers? Why am I more at home in dense forests than in crowded malls? Where did my fascination with the mysteries of nature come from and why is there this urgency to write about it?

This spring, smiling down on those young seedlings, I make a pledge to spend more than just a few moments with my rural rooted beginnings. This season I decide to reacquaint myself with the faint but enduring memories, to capture the voices once heard in country fields and to shape into verse the wisdom shared with me by those who were true harvesters of life. This year I'll take time to honor the truth I uncover when I step into my garden on those too-early-in-the-spring days.

———

Chase Road

It was no more than a mile long
from end to end –
our home planted square in the middle –
making it possible
on school holidays and on my one speed bike
to call on all the wonders
of that vibrant world.

My first stop was always right next door,
at Grandma's garden,
where I walked alongside her
as she taught me the homegrown secrets
of knowing worth from weed.
Later we'd step into the chicken coop
to gather the day's eggs or
to grab a plump hen, axe off its head
and watch
as it ran the life out of itself.

Across the road was a farm family.
Ten boys filled that homestead –
assurance I'd never want for a playmate.
We jumped from barn lofts onto haystacks,
learned about life from the birthing cows,
and awakened to something bigger than us
in the open fields.

My uncle's mucklands
lay down the road a stretch.
He employed me,
at the ripe old age of eight,
to top onions for ten cents a bushel.
By the end of the day
I was rich with change in my pocket

and with a change in myself:
a working man now.

And all along the way
there were woods and streams to explore
offering a kind of quiet
unheard of today
and rising from it
a voice
eager to tell of all the wonders found
in my Chase Road world.

Beginnings

Grownup heads scraped the ceiling.
Flimsy walls whistled with the wind.
The dirt-streaked window was stingy
with sunlight. But it was there
on Gramma's back porch
that the farmer in me was born ~

Beans sorted & snipped,
chickens plucked & deboned,
farm gossip sifted & preserved.
And on my favorite day,
popping corn was harvested,
the dried cobs stripped
by a thumbnail pressed hard
up and down each golden row.

At 3 years old,
I would sit across from her
working the husks 'til my hands blistered,
the calluses on my fingers
a wise investment made
so that I might become
just like her.

Other children were eager
to run 'round the bases
or to enliven a doll's house.
I found my happiness
on this back porch,
both hands
          grabbing hold of life.

Settling

With each bump
this tractor reminds me I should be awake.
It's early Saturday,
there's a day of topping ahead of me
and I'm stalling.

Uncle Sam is at the wheel,
his migrant worker sitting beside him
dropping stacks of bushels at the head of each row.
I know I should jump off –
any row will do –
but I'm enjoying this ride:
the steady putt putt of the tractor
  composing a muckland lullaby,
the multilingual chatter of these two men
  hashing out plans for the day,
the ease of machinery
  moving me through time and space.

Why would I want to trade this
for a pair of topping shears
and the stench of onion in every breath?

Uncle warns
You better get started
and I leap,
my boots sinking into muck,
the tractor fading into quiet.

Dropping to my knees
I drag myself to the start of a row,
grab 3 or 4 onions by their limp, ribboned tops,
and snip them over a bushel.
Tumbling into place
   they piece together the crisp notes
      of a new melody,
         one I will listen to
            a few thousand times today.

Muckland Meditation

It is here I learn the word endless –
  plowed fields as far as the eye can see,
    black with potential.
      And I, a dot on this earthen map,
        navigate its richness,
          row by row.

  Blue sky matches the muck's vastness
    eyeful for eyeful.
      Its canopy lovingly "has my back"
        as I come to trust
          its sun
            and rain
              and stillness.

The occasional bird calls out,
  pecking through that silence,
    his soliloquies
      lilting from the treetops,
        each song telling a story.

Those stories encircle my solitude,
  cradle me in my youth.
    From here I will grow
      strong and vital,
        from here I will discover
          the fertile soil
            of a quiet soul.

Melon Jolly

Just across the road
farm fields spread to the horizon,
making the view from our living room window
grand.
Each August
miles of watermelon vines
became a meandering picture show,
admired but not to be entered –
such a view the livelihood
of a farmer across the way.

But every once in a while,
the day at its peak,
that farmer's son would call over,
inviting us to meet him in those melon fields.
We'd dash cross the road and each choose one –
the smaller, rounder variety best
for young hands.

Finding a pointy boulder
we'd crack that sphere open,
red juice baptizing our bare arms and blue jeans.
Then,
sitting cross-legged atop warm soil,
we'd raise those crooked smiles of green
to our own thirsty grins,
tempering the heat of country living,
sharing a delicious pause in the drone of the day,
discovering,
                  quite early in life,
            how it is we go about
                  growing
                  our own joy.

Stumbling Upon The Old Creek

Are you still my meandering waters?
Favorite play toy of my childhood,
unvisited all these years:
water spilling over your stones in forest symphonies,
your deep pockets bubbling with elusive tadpoles,
my eager arms diving through you
stirring up treasures
found below.

Or are you some channel to my redemption?
Deliverance dreamed of
and discovered at last:
gazing into your churning waters that do not lie,
expecting a middle aged cheerless reflection,
startled by
a ten year old forest faery
rippling
in and out.

No matter
if you are history
or foreshadowing
I hold handfuls of your depths
close to my face
and breathe in
the DNA
of my essence.

About Muck and Me

It is the richest soil found on earth.
Its primary ingredient is rotting vegetation.

It is an ideal environment for growing the nutritious foods we
consume.
It is a breeding ground for an array of grubs and insects.

It is home to the seed which bursts to life under long hours of
brilliant sunshine.
It must spend equally long hours under the darkness of snow
before it is ready for seed.

It is more valuable than gold to the serious farmer.
It must be thoroughly scrubbed off his boots before he's
allowed in his home.

This is why I love it so.

I love having my feet planted in two such different worlds:
the royalty and the rubbish.

I love how it informs my dichotomous life,
one often spent in a tug-a-war of conflicting truths.

I love that something outside me reflects
that which is inside me.

Family Matters

Some days I remember being born and raised in a family of six. Other days, I'd say it was more like sixty. There was, of course, my family of a dad and mom, brother and sisters, but just as surely, there was my family of grandparents, cousins, aunts, uncles, godparents, and that unique member of the mix referred to by Italians as "*compare:*" anyone not a blood relative or married into the clan, but who had somehow found themselves threaded into the family fabric.

Being part of a big or small family isn't really a choice when you grow up a descendant of immigrated farmers. Family is sacred to immigrants and the bigger the better. I know this from listening to stories of my grandparents who, at tender ages, left behind their families to travel to America, many of them never seeing their loved ones again. Arriving in a new land, after finding shelter and employment, their most important task was to recreate the sense of love and community held in their hearts from the homeland. With traditions and life lessons from the old country, they began the task of building a new history – from scratch.

My extended family not only gathered at weddings and funerals but also was there for the more commonplace home repairs and had-to-be-tried recipes, car troubles and school recitals, dog bites and first dates. My memories of a typical day in my childhood go something like this: I've gotten on Mom's nerves for the 10th time today, so I sneak over to Gramma's for some homemade bread and unconditional loving. Later, my brother goes off to baseball practice and I'm bored, so I call over a cousin or two and head down to the creek to try our hand at out-jumping the frogs. Or maybe I'd gotten into some sort of trouble and Dad's not around for a lesson-learning kick in the butt. Any uncle's foot will do just fine.

How rich and full life was with people who cared so much and could assume so many family roles. One fall a killing frost was predicted, threatening my Uncle's ready-to-be-harvested onion crop. Early the next morning the whole family pulled on old clothes and hit the fields, working quickly to save as many onions as we could from the life sapping freeze. We were each other's Peace Corps, Salvation Army, Habitat For Humanity. We were the always open soup kitchen, the doctor who made house calls.

I observed each member of my family as they took seed, sprouted, budded and burst, then watched as they faded and returned to the earth. Over the years each of them had a starring role in my version of what *The Reader's Digest* calls "My Most Unforgettable Character," and now that my recollections are nearly a half century old they seem far too important to keep to myself. Not only are these memories woven into my family's fabric but also into the fabric of a young, aspiring America: these stories of a humble immigrant family, some with six characters, some with sixty.

Grand(pa) Memory

Snapshot:
A shovelful of snow sails across the sky.
It flies up and over tall snow banks
that have made our long driveway
into a frozen tunnel,
carved out
by a tiny powerhouse of a man:
my seventy year old grandpa
working hard
in the winter of 1958.

A few miles down the road
and fifty-two winters beyond that memory,
I attack my own driveway,
clearing it –
not with our modern-day snowblower –
but with my own two hands,
modeling myself on this weathered recollection
of Grandpa ~

This is all I remember of him –
me, so new to the world and
him, so near his last days –
but I've taken that memory far,
using it as a template for how to live my life:
how to chip away at my ambitions,
how to dig for my successes –
never stopping
'til a job is done.

A Slice Of Life

We watch
as she gently picks up that loaf of homemade Italian bread,
still warm from her Old World oven,
its mouth-watering aroma filling us
with promise.

She holds that loaf in one hand,
steadies it against her ribcage,
its brown crust glowing
atop a faded patterned housedress.

Her other hand holds a sharpened bread knife
and she begins sawing through that loaf
one - two - three times
each slice of the knife
stopping precariously close to her body ~

We always worried
one day her knife will slip
and she'd cut off a breast
which,
we also were certain,
she would have sacrificed for us:
her grandchildren,
her lineage,
her purpose for opening and closing each day
in that farmhouse life she led.

Frozen Treat

Here you are
making miracles again:
stretching our garden hose
so out of season
across the January snow,
feeding a pond mushrooming
in the side yard.
We're all screaming:
Now, Dad? Now?

You answer with your steady silence,
eyes on your task,
cigarette dangling between determined lips.

We busy ourselves
   rebuilding then ambushing snow forts,
      filling the yard with families of snow angels,
         hide-and-seeking among the naked lilac bushes.

Now, Dad?

Finally,
after supper and a dry pair of socks,
we strap on our blades.
In darkness
we stumble across crusted snowdrifts
and step onto
our very own ice skating rink –

winter suddenly fresh as the first snow.
You kids,
Mom says,
the luckiest Eskimos in the neighborhood.

Tap

Night surrounds me.

There are no streetlights on our country road
to offer even a ray of comfort
through my window,
no blanket of warm light
spread across my bed.
Tummy aches hurt all the more
endured in this forever darkness.

                    Then I remember
the tap on the wall
you told me I could always make
when I needed you.
When I do
you are here
like magic
and,
in just your being so,
my tummy settles
and the darkness too.

Blizzard

We lived for a week under its spell.
The world looked too tall
too white
and the grownups proclaimed it too much
so we let it be

and pulled out the card table –
staging marathon Monopoly matches,
killing each other at War
and making up our own rules for Rummy.
All of us –
the streamlets of our family –
pooled together
inside this deep freeze.

We ventured outside now and then,
sliding off the roof,
sending snowballs up and over telephone wires
but never getting past the driveway
'til Dad got stir crazy,
made snowshoes out of old planks and twine
and walked to the dairy.
Mom got creative with the dinner menu
and served cup after cup of hot cocoa.
Each day drifted sweetly
into the next

'til the plow came
and shattered that precious snowglobe,
the card table folded up
and we rivers rambled out
                          and away.

Divining

My uncle walks our stretch of land
holding a Y shaped branch,
gripping one point in each hand,
with the third
aiming forward.
He moves slowly…
ceremonially.
No one says a word.

Back and forth he wanders,
letting the limb lead him
until urgently
it draws straight down.
Here,
his knowing finger points,
Dig down 13 feet.

Dad – never an easy believer –
brings in a second uncle.
Different man, same slip of a stick.

A few hours later,
at 13 feet,
we find the waters we seek.
Dad shakes each uncle's hand

while I quake in the mystery –
from that day forward
keeping an eye out for magic –
never needing more than one time
to believe.

Market Value

4 AM.
He gives my shoulder a light shake
and a gruff *Time to get up*.
We climb into the truck,
already loaded the night before,
and its headlights weave a path
from this still sleeping farm
to the Saturday morning market
in the city.

My job is to wait on customers:
emptying baskets of onions into paper sacks,
shaking dirt off heads of iceberg lettuce,
and making change,
showing off my 5th grade smarts.
The pace is fast
and I never notice the predawn darkness becoming
a day so bright.

The dollars he folds at the end of the morning
are his living,
the months of toiling his farmlands
come down to this weekly exchange.
Tomorrow,
when he's back at it on the mucks,
his family will kneel and pray for sunny Saturdays,
for bustling market crowds.

On the way home
we stop at the hotdog stand
and he buys me two coneys
and a soda –
a few dollars thinned off his profit –
but a happy ending for me, his nephew,
who never said a proper thank you
for showing me that marketplace pulse of life –
that day I got to dive right in and be
part of the flow.

'Compare' John

He lived down our country road
on a large onion farm
and,
a relative of a relative,
he gave me my first job.
I worked alongside him,
stripping the brown and spent tops
that once gave life
to those plump, potent bulbs.
The work seemed endless
and the hours were silent
   save for the rattling of the onions
   tumbling to their place in the bushel

   and John's trademark whistle:
the same note
over and over
and over again,
searching

       like a cricket's lonely plea

          or some galaxy-exploring radio signal.

Simple and strange I used to think.

Happy in life I now imagine.

Stepping Down

A grown daughter on each arm,
she is being led through the rooms of her house,
her belongings packed in suitcases and boxes,
piled into the line of cars,
waiting.

She mouths
in private Italian
her good-bye to each bare room,
steps down onto the porch
and,
like the weary and burdened traveler,
she can carry herself no further.
Her daughters hold strong,
keeping her on this uncharted course

for they are the leaders of the family now

something they –
something all of us –
never expected
would come to be.

Aunt Francis

She never learned to drive a car
but life took her for some amazing rides.
Some she welcomed
but more than a few
just showed up
unbidden.

There was, of course,
the two children she raised,
the farmhouse she kept
and the way she held the center
of our sprawling family.

But what about the 20 years of care
she devoted to her failed, arthritic mother?

What about opening the porch door
to find her husband
collapsed on the stairs,
tractor accident slamming that chapter closed?

And what about the stroke,
first taking her left side,
then her smile,
then her mind?

We've all –
the generation that came from hers –
vacationed in foreign countries,
sat center row for Broadway shows,
explored our curiosities in cyberspace.
But none of us
ever dug our heels into life
like she did.

———

Leotta's Barn

I got word that the old barn collapsed.
Strong winds.
Heavy snows.
  Deep memories ~

  Us boys
tired and hungry after a long day topping,
and old 'Compare' John,
bent and crotchety,
offering us, in Italian-laced English,
rhubarb dipped in sugar
like it was some nectar of the gods.
We turn up our nose
at such a strange refreshment
and such a foreign, pitiful man.

  In the house is his wife, 'Comare' Nellie,
a small, spirited woman,
with less English than John
but more the welcoming.
First you had to get past her dog, Tippie,
who would *yip! yip! yip!* at you
'til Nellie yipped back: *Tippie!*
Then you'd sit at her table downing a cold glass of lemonade
and,
if the day was right,
a piece of leftover birthday cake.
Nellie would wrap nickels & dimes in foil
and drop them in cake batter,
and somebody's lucky slice made them a rich man.

Both of them
gone more than 30 years,
  and now,

among the barn's broken, rotted timbers,
I find my scattered recollections
both sweet and bitter:
like sugar on the rhubarb,
like lemons
floating in the sweet waters of time.

The World A Bit Quieter

Outside the church
strains of a pipe organ
grow loud then soft
as the heavy doors release us
one grieving group at a time.

Off to the side gather the farmers,
weathered by their lives,
trading stories and paying respects to one of their own
taken by a freak tractor accident.

He was 68 years old
but you never would have known it:
muscles ballooned and supple,
tanned face reflecting the mucklands
that called to him each morning.

We nieces and nephews knew him as a jolly man,
always with a joke to top off Sunday dinners,
our favorite Santa Claus each Christmas Eve,
and those elfin eyes punctuating his far fetched stories ~

Surprisingly the world went on
but part of the passion that went into each growing season
was buried with him,
and the farming life
never held such promise again.

Intertwined

Soon it will be time:
       One crisp mid-winter morning
        I'll look out my kitchen window,
         deem the day perfect,
          grab garden snippers,
           plow through snowdrifts
            and stand before my stretch
                                of tangled grapevine.

I'll know just what to do:
  I learned it from my father,
   who learned it from my grandmother,
   who carried it from Italy to America,
    the lessons of her sixteen years and
     a slice of root from her Papa's vine
            close to heart.

I'll pause before making my first cut and think about this
twisting history:
  How my grapevine is vibrant proof of my ancestors,
   how its root, lodged so deeply in my soil,
    is a great grandchild of what burrowed in theirs.
   Some of their long ago lives I know by heart,
    while others remain
        elusive and mysterious.

Before my work is done I'll welcome one more mystery:
  With each clip of the vine
   I'll get a whiff of grape essence and
   – if the sun hits it just right –
    a tiny bubble of sap will rise at the cut,
     shimmering, like a single tear,
      reflecting the entwinement of a family
     that bears, for me,
        such sweet fruit.

Piecing Together My Day/My Life

Today I cooked up a batch of soup, a warm weekly ritual that nourishes me throughout the winter season. As I was peeling the onions, tears rose, as one would expect from handling that headiest of vegetables. But today the tears were more than a knee jerk reaction to some chemical unleashed in its slicing. They rose from the richness that this reliving of my history has provided me. Peeling down through the layers of my life, poem by poem, has brought a new, contented perspective about my earliest years and my tears are droplets of thanks.

As the soup simmers I finish packing my suitcase, getting ready to head for Michigan, where my daughter lives. She's part of a special ceremony at her church and we'll all be there: her mother, our son, his girlfriend and me. Our family, though fragmented and scattered around the country, will come together for these few days. As hard as it is to leave my home so early in the growing season – each day the backyard is a showcase of awakening – family calls, and the time spent revisiting my history tells me there is no greater call to heed.

Before I sit down to my first bowlful of soup I play a quiet melody on the piano: *Both Sides Now*, that Joni Mitchell classic; its poignant lyric haunting me more with each listening:

I've looked at life from both sides now
from win and lose and still somehow
it's life's illusions I recall
I really don't know life at all... *

*Siquomb Publishing Company

Joni wrote this song as a teenager and I am in awe at how she made such an insightful observation at that tender age. It would be many years beyond my teens before I was brave enough to look at my life's mysteries. *My* teen years were spent plowing through each day, moving further from my rural roots, hoping that by abandoning that simple country culture, I could also leave behind all it was that confused me.

As the day draws to its end I find a few moments to work on my poems. The time spent with them, like time with a trusted friend, has helped me reconsider what have always been small, vague moments of my childhood. They are among the stories brought up at family reunions, smiled about, then easily packed away and forgotten. But by shaping them into verse they have led me to a greater understanding. Like those tiny sprouts I see each spring, long hidden under winter's darkness, these poems become the forerunners of who it is I have gladly become.

As Good As Red

We're packed into the living room on a Saturday night,
relatives visiting.
The box in the corner is warming up
and our fingers are crossed
hoping that its antenna cooperates
and brings welcome relief
to this burdened family.

It's Red Skelton night
and that means we will laugh –
out loud.
Pound-the-arm-of-the-chair-gasp-for-breath kind of laughs
passed round the room,
like Good Humor candy,
too delicious to ever want to stop.

After the show
I do my imitation of Red
imitating his favorite two seagulls:
fingers under armpits,
elbows flapping.
The grownups stop their card game
and laugh some more at their youngest –

who imagines he is that TV star,
who dreams that,
if he gets Red down real good,
he can keep their laughter going
beyond the hour
                    beyond Saturday night
laughter like oxygen,
keeping us giddily alive.

Moment

I am no taller than the apron strings
tied round my Aunt's waist
waving in the early morning breeze.
She and Mom say I'm old enough this year
so they take me along –
back beyond the barn
to where open fields meet the forest,
where bushes hold purple pearls
of sweetness.

Hanging from a thin string
round my neck,
my bucket fills.
I reach up and collect a handful
in a moment's time,
dreaming about the muffins and pies
that will crown our feast at family picnics –
so I pop a few in my mouth
taste testing that kinship and contentment ~

I don't remember
how long we worked
or how many buckets I filled.
Those are the kinds of details that leave.

But what stays
is the peace of that memory
which I have kept right here
– in my heart-bucket –
for all the times I've needed to taste
again
a blueberry moment.

At The Beach

You look new to me
in your dark blue bathing suit,
so much more skin
then the clean-shaven serious face
poking out of a business suit
rushing through our kitchen
each morning.

And look how your smile stays
as you show us water tricks,
squirting geysers from your cupped hands
or floating on your back,
feet pulled in close to your head
(*Look kids! I'm a midget!*).
We laugh
and beg for turns riding on your back –
we are dolphins first,
then Superman's cape.
Holding tight,
my nose pressed to your neck,
I breathe in the lake water washing over your aftershave –
each inhalation
heady.

Mom calls us out of the water.
No! we cry.
Just one more ride, Dad!
One more water trick!
One more real moment

with this
silly
happy version
of my Dad.

Woolworths

It was there
> Mrs. Robarge marched in
> six of her proud 2nd graders
> to cash in our perfect attendance awards
> for a tall glass of Coca-Cola
> served up at the lunch counter.
> Six fannies sat on those counter swivel seats,
> bottom halves doing the twist
> while our top halves drank in
> the pulsating store life
> as we savored our colas and our luck.

It was there
> my best friend met me one Saturday in the pet aisle
> and, as we watched fish swim round the aquariums,
> he told me how babies were made,
> his sketchy details churning up questions
> as colorful as the exotic species
> darting before me.
> I tried to picture my father and mother
> swimming round the fishbowl of their bedroom
> making my baby sister,
> life suddenly as uncharted as tropical waters.

And it was there
> Dad gave us ten dollars each
> one Christmas Eve afternoon
> and set us loose to find gifts worthy of a spot
> beneath the family tree.
> No trinket was left unturned
> as we counted and recounted our five and dimes,
> stretching our love far:
> our own Christmas miracle cradled
> in shopping baskets and hopeful hearts.

It's a Dollar Store now.
        I never go in.
        They don't carry what I'd be looking for.

The Saloon

Somebody nicknamed it the Beauty Saloon
and it became a running family joke.
It was my aunt's in-home shop,
and Mom helped out –
a second set of hands fiddling
with ladies' hair, combing
through the gossip.
We kids weren't allowed in
but the nearby TV room
got me close enough to be swallowed up
by the roar of hair dryers,
the rinse water gurgling down pipes,
the ladies foraging purses for bills and coins.
       There was comfort in the orderliness of it all.

The day Kennedy was shot
we were released from school early.
Mom was at the Saloon
and I went straight there,
walking the streets
numb
in a world without a President.

I knew if I could just get to my Aunt's
things would be right again
but I arrived to discover
the bustle of the ladies
drawn,
the talk
darker.
From the TV room
I watched Oswald gunned down by Jack Ruby
live.
In an instant
heads, rollered and bobby pinned,
left the Saloon
and surrounded me,
all of us
fixed to the screen –
      Life never to hold its permanence again.

Aftertaste

It's why every piece of chocolate,
no matter how sweet,
leaves a trace of regret...

Sneaking onto their back porch,
you gingerly twist the kitchen doorknob.
A ray of light angles out
and we walk through it.

They sit in their living room
watching some Saturday night variety show –
her laugh, the eternal child's,
his, a cynical man's.
  They're hard of hearing,
  you whisper,
  There's nothing to worry about.

We tip toe to the fridge
wait for more laughter
then open the door
and fill our pockets with handfuls
of wrapped bars.
Then 1 2 3
        we cross the kitchen
            slip the door to its frame
                and jump off the porch.

Their laughter rises again:
now a departing train
emptying into the night.

They'll never miss them,
you say,
unwrapping one.
They've pretty much lost their minds.
I nod,
taking my first bitter bite.

Migrating

They work hard on this onion farm,
these dark-skinned men,
darker than all the shades of my family and friends –
a darkness
that enlightens my life.

I work alongside them
but not among them.
They tower closer to the sky
and smell deeply of the earth.
When they speak
their words crackle with life –
voices sizzling in anger
or cascading with laughter.
Their talk is otherworldly,
a mysterious code I want to crack.

At break-time they cluster together
ladling cool water into parched, pink mouths
and onto perspiring heads of midnight black curls.
Thin streams cut through the muck dust
that coats their shirtless solid torsos.

My Uncle interrupts their chatter with instructions for the next
chore.
He sees these men as a necessity to running his farm.
I see them as a foreign brotherhood
off limits to me, but
how happy I am
sharing this muckland,
these men showing me
a complexion
that awaits
beyond my pale little world.

—

Eyes of Grace

We are gathered at Gramma's
where, for the first time since leaving Italy at 16,
she has been reunited with her sister,
Grace.
The whole family congregates on the front lawn,
thank the Lord that the weather cooperated –
sun and a cooling breeze
blessing this sacred occasion.

We kids are marched up, one by one
to our guest –
Grace, with her limited English
and us, nary a word of Italian.
Our aunt translates a two or three sentence bio about each of
us:
a few details to help tell one from another.
I walk tentatively toward her and stand –
strange that a relative could seem
like a stranger.

Then our eyes meet:
hers
filled with pilgrimage
and deep
with the wonder of this reunion

and mine
nervous of what she would think of my bio,
and shallow
with not a word to offer –
surprised to find
that the yearning for family
adjoining our eyes
would say it all.

Ripe

We walked through your lush vegetable garden
as you shared with me,
beyond the barrier of language,
a collected wisdom
about the wonders of that green expansive world.

My intrigue with your world
has held fast a half century now.
You've been dead thirty of those years but,
like a miracle,
you go on living.

Your greatest gift
came to me in a dream –
one that haunts and excites me still –
the way our best dreams always do:

> You and I are one person
> walking through that fertile garden
> carrying a watermelon too big for our slight arms.
> We are the Italian immigrant
> searching this fertile land for a better life.
> We are the wayfaring grandson
> searching, too, for a place to belong.
> We are pleading as one voice:
> *Help me*
> *I can't carry this all by myself!*

The melon falls to the ground
smashing to pieces
revealing –
as a broken life sometimes does –

our ripe and luscious possibilities.

Ode

To this mucklands boy
    humming a tune sung by those who tended the fields,
    words long ago lost
    but its melody
    rooted.

To this backwoods boy
    recalling his forest-sprite days,
    abandoned for a right angled life
    which,
    he comes to find,
    does not work.

To this brook-spirit boy
    riding the waters that carve our destiny,
    having been over his head
    a time or two but
    of late
    afloat.

For this country boy
    re-emerging like spring time,
    the world anew
    through reflections of old,
    for him I offer
    this humble
          joyful
            welcome.

About the Author

Jim Farfaglia has always lived in the northeastern United States, never far from farmland or backyard gardens. For many years he ran Camp Hollis, which is located on the shores of Lake Ontario and he is the co-author of the pictorial essay: *Camp Hollis, The Origins Of Oswego County's Children's Camp.* Jim currently lives in Fulton, New York, just a short distance from his childhood home.

10444854R00034

Made in the USA
Charleston, SC
05 December 2011